W9-BWS-993

Hetty and Harriet

Graham Oakley

Atheneum   New York

Copyright © 1981 by Graham Oakley
All rights reserved
Library of Congress catalog card number: 81–8024
ISBN: 0–689–30888–4
First American Edition 1982
Printed in Great Britain by Sackville Press, Billericay

On a farm by a river
lived several chickens.
The youngest of these
chickens was named
Hetty, and because she
was the youngest all
the other chickens
pecked her. But Hetty
didn't mind because she had a hazy
notion that she wouldn't always be the
youngest.

The next youngest chicken was named
Harriet, and because she was the next
youngest all the other chickens except
one pecked her. But Harriet *did* mind.
She said all the hens were jealous and

Alfred the cockerel was
just a bad tempered
show-off. As well as
that, she said the farm
was dreary, the food
boring, her roost drafty
and the barnyard dirty.

Every day Harriet told Hetty,
"Just over there is a wonderful place
where everything's perfect. One day I'll
run away and live there, and even though
you're young and silly I'll take you with
me." Every day Hetty would say, "Ooo,
how nice," and then forget all about it.

Then one night there was a terrible storm, and the next morning
when the chickens were let out a strange sight met their eyes.

To all the other hens it meant lots and lots of worms and caterpillars and grubs and lovely things like that.
But Harriet said to Hetty that it was the Pathway to a New Life. Hetty rather agreed with the other hens but she didn't say anything.

Harriet joined in and had a jolly good breakfast just the same. Then she told Hetty that the time had come to depart for the place 'just over there' where everything was *perfect*. Hetty thought everything was perfect where they were but she said to herself, "I'm young and silly and she must know best," and she followed Harriet quietly.

They reached the other bank and spent a very pleasant morning. There was earth to scratch in and dust to have dust baths in and all kinds of delicacies to be found. But, best of all, there was now no one to peck Harriet,

and only one to peck Hetty. But after a while Harriet started to notice a few little things she didn't like about the place, and as the day wore on they grew into a lot of large things she didn't like. By roosting time she was very grumpy indeed and pecked Hetty for not having anything to say for herself, for being too talkative, for having white feathers and for being too young, and when she ran out of reasons she pecked her for nothing at all. Next morning she awoke Hetty with a peck just as the sun was rising and cried, "Look! Just over there! It's the *perfect* place for us."

It took them quite a long time to reach the spot they'd seen from the tree, but when they did they both thought it had been well worth the trouble. "It's the *perfect* spot, just as I said," cried Harriet. "And look, there's even a cosy little place to sleep in." Each of the hens bustled about and made herself a snug nest, and as they settled down for a well-earned rest Harriet murmured drowsily, "Peace, perfect peeaaahhhHHH ..." Hetty often wondered afterwards what she had been going to say.

"Why on earth did you have to pick a place like that?" gasped Harriet. Hetty couldn't remember, but she thought it must have been because she wasn't as old and as clever as Harriet. At last they came to a place which Harriet thought was absolutely perfect, and they passed the rest of the day enjoying themselves finding grubs and things like that. They even found corn in the nooks and crannies, but Harriet said it was a bit 'off'. When evening came they went into the windmill and, bearing the fox in mind, climbed to the top floor and roosted there.

But when it got dark and the moon came out they began seeing very strange and frightening things.

In the end they had to scramble out on to the sails for safety. "I don't know why you wanted to stay in this horrible place," grumbled Harriet. Hetty was just trying to remember why when Harriet shrieked, "Look, just over there! All those beautiful bright lights. It's the *perfect* place for us."

The town was a lot further off than it had looked and they lost their way a few times, so it was dark before they arrived and they had to put up with a makeshift roost that night.

Next morning they set off to explore but they found the place rather disappointing. It was hours before they came across somewhere to scratch, and that wasn't much of a place either. And even then they weren't left in peace for long. In fact there was such a furore that they could have been committing a crime or something. Harriet said, as they fled for their lives, that obviously all the world was against chickens.

There were pickings to be had, but they felt that the company was a bit low. Hetty was quite happy to swallow her pride if she could swallow a few other things besides, but Harriet made such a fuss about who ate what before whom that they were shoo-ed off with their bellies still empty.

Later on they tried a change of diet. But they really weren't given time to find out whether they liked it or not. So after that they were reduced to looking for scraps in the street, like any common scavenger.

There wasn't much to be found in the road, and anyway everybody was so impatient. The shouting and the hooting of horns grew so deafening that the two hens got very flustered and just ran around in circles. But everything was sorted out in the end.

Their home was really quite comfortable. The food was good and it was very warm and cosy. Even Harriet said it would do for the moment, though it was far from perfect. As for Hetty, she thought it was heavenly. But like most good things, it didn't last long.

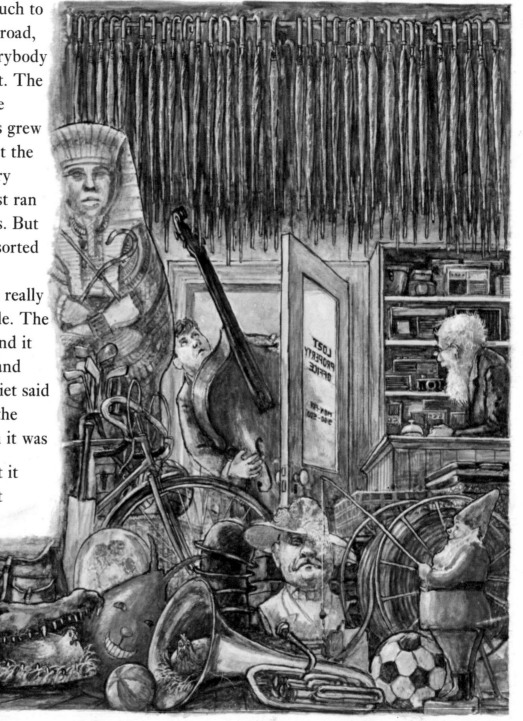

Harriet was very optimistic during the short journey to their new home. She said she felt in her bones that it would be *perfect*. It was rather nice and Hetty loved it right from the start, even though everybody still pecked her. But everybody except one still pecked Harriet, and she hated it.

One evening as they were scratching on the ash heap just before they were shut up for the night, Harriet cried suddenly, "Look, just over there! It's the *perfect* place for us."

So early next morning they crept away, and after a long walk they came to the spot Harriet had seen. "There you are," she cried. "Look how modern and shiny it is. It's the absolutely *perfect* place for us."

Harriet couldn't wait to get into the place, and it didn't take long to find a way.

"Ooo, it's just as wonderful as I thought it would be," cried Harriet. "Look how clean it is. How warm and cosy, everybody in their own little room. And look at all the food and how bright the lights are. How lucky all these chickens are to have such a lovely home. I wish we could live here."

And the words were scarcely out of her mouth before the wish was granted.

For the first ten minutes Harriet liked her little room. After another ten minutes she didn't like it. Ten minutes after that she absolutely hated it. "I can't think why you wanted to leave our last home," she said to Hetty. Hetty couldn't either, so she kept quiet. As that seemed to be the end of that

conversation, Harriet turned to the hen on the other side and said in a chatty kind of way that it was nice weather for the time of year. The hen replied irritably that she didn't have time for silly gossip because she had her daily quota of eggs to lay, and if Harriet knew what was good for her she would do the same. Harriet said huffily that she didn't lay eggs to order for anybody.

After that there was nothing for Harriet to do but think her own thoughts.

And there was nothing for Hetty to do but think hers. Every day a man looked at each cage and made notes. In front of some he looked grim. In front of Harriet and Hetty he looked very grim indeed, and shook his head as well. Then one day he looked even grimmer than usual, and soon after that things started to happen.

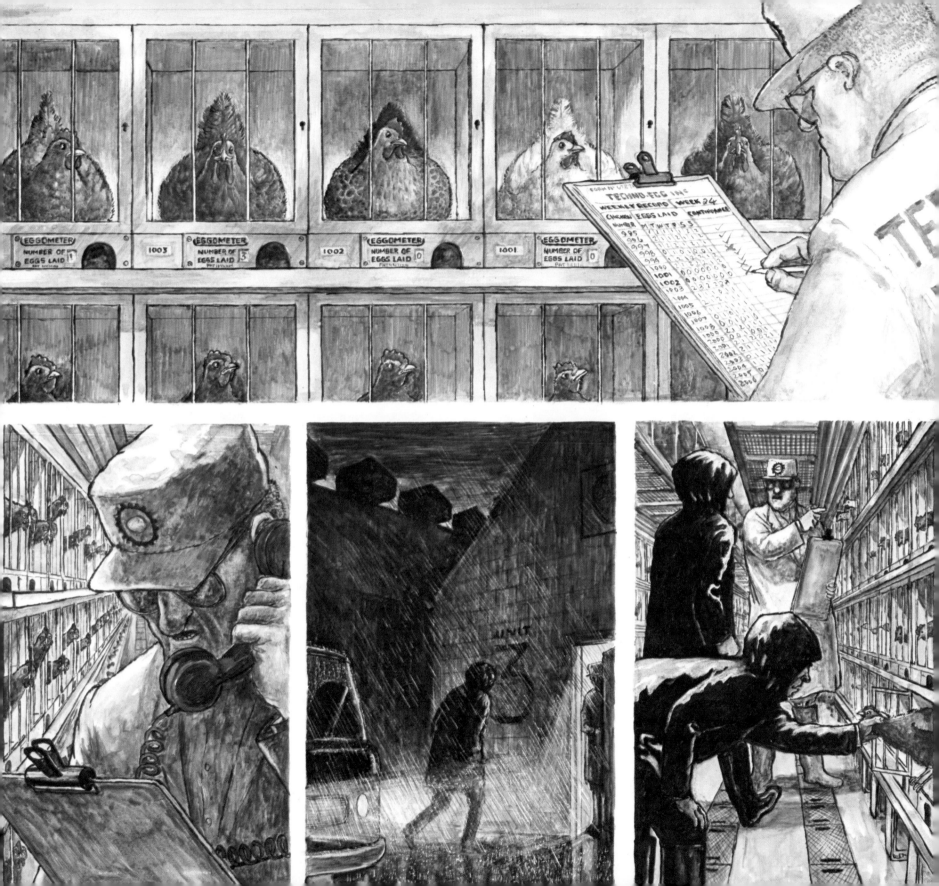

Harriet had decided that there couldn't be a worse place than their present home, but as they were marched out she started to think that perhaps there could be.

But she tried to be cheery. As they climbed into the van she said in a quavery voice, "I expect where we are g-g-going will be *p-p-p-perfect*." But when they were bundled out at the journey's end any such idea died within her. After one look at that dreadful place she knew that if they entered it they would never come out.

So, quick as lightning, Harriet acted …

and then, as quick as lightning, Hetty acted …

… and then, as quick as lightning, everybody acted. When they were sure they were safe from pursuit they stopped to get their breath back. Then Harriet said, "Come on Hetty, we must be pushing on." They said goodbye to the other hens and set off, rather guiltily, by themselves.

But then something came over Hetty. She forgot that she was young and silly, and she cried, "I won't go another step without the others. What will they do without us, poor dears, they have led sheltered lives." To Hetty's surprise Harriet just said, "Oh, all right then." That was because she was feeling guilty about leaving them too.

So they all went off together. Nobody knew where to, but Harriet said that it would be the *perfect* place for them. At first they got wet ...

... then they got tired ...

... then they got cold ...

... then they got nervous ...

... then they got frightened ...

... then they got terrified ...

... and then they ran out of the bushes and saw that they were trapped and that there was no hope for them.

The hens were frantic. To escape
those terrible teeth for just a few more
seconds they scrambled out on the pieces of driftwood,
flapping their wings in terror as they
went. Then a strange thing happened. It took
Harriet a few moments to grasp it, then she shrieked,
"Flap as hard as you can." And in a matter of seconds
they were safe. Soon they were clucking and
chattering with relief, and telling
each other that they hadn't
been frightened at all really,
when suddenly Harriet
screeched, "Look, just over
there! It's definitely the most absolutely *perfect* possible place for us! I knew I would find it one day.
We'll all be happy for ever and ever there." And as soon as she saw the place, Hetty, even though she was
young and silly, knew that Harriet was right at last.